She turned me into the Abominable Snowman!
Although I like being called "Yeti" better.

Just for that, I turned her into Frogzilla!

So she turned me into Princess Stinkerbell.

Then I changed her into a Scottish Gargyle!

We were so busy turning each other into crazy creatures that we didn't notice...

...my Think-a-ma-Jink
got knocked into the air...

...and smashed
into a **million
bajillion pieces!**

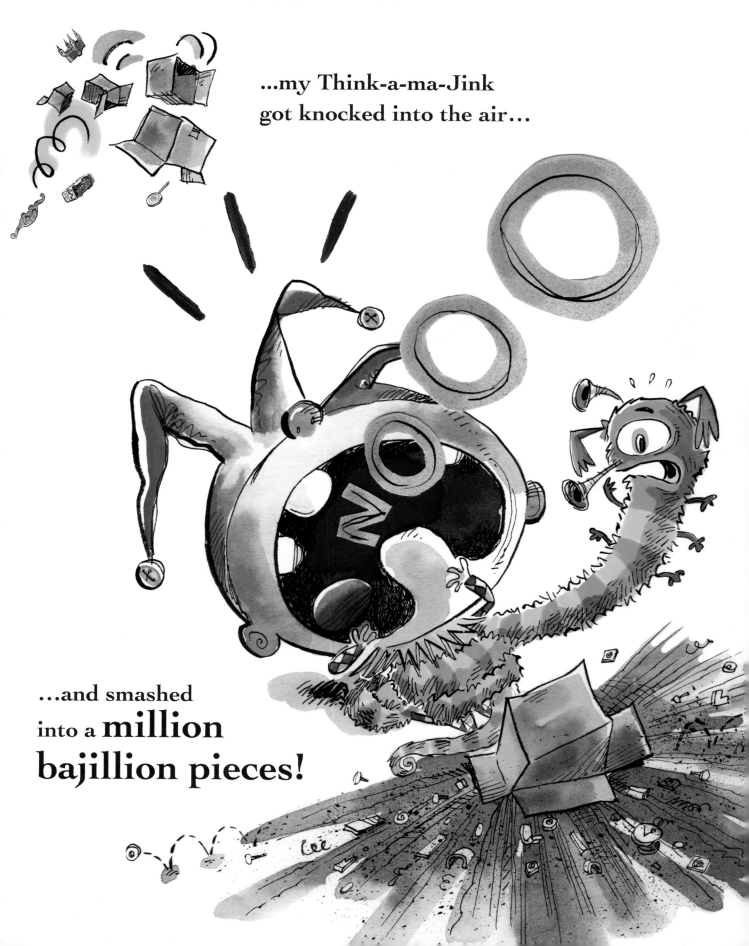

This couldn't be happening!

Not the Think-a-ma-Jink!

What about my adventures?

What should I do?

I had to think!

It worked! I actually did it **all by myself!**

And if I could do THAT...